Praise for
A Child's Christmas in Williamsburg

"Joseph Nicolello's *A Child's Christmas in Williamsburg* is a multifaceted gem. Part panegyric to New York City, part celebration of the most beloved time of the liturgical year, part paean to the enchanted world of childhood wherein one's dreams can and do come true, the novella charms readers with the poignant story of seven-year-old Sarah and her mother as they celebrate their first Christmas together after divorce. Nicolello captures the electric energy of New York, the air of wild expectation, and the boundless promise Christmas holds out for humankind—all made manifest in the yearnings of a child for the simplest of gifts: faith, hope, and love. In the great tradition of Dylan Thomas, Isak Dinesan, and Betty Smith, *A Child's Christmas* offers us a luminous portrait of imperfect people in an imperfect place pondering the impossible perfection that every now and then miraculously becomes ours."

—ANGELA ALAIMO O'DONNELL, author of *Still Pilgrim* (Paraclete 2017) and *Andalusian Hours: Poems from the Porch of Flannery O'Connor* (Paraclete 2020)

"A charming New York Christmas story of the hardship and love of a seven-year-old girl and her mother. They are unaware that the material gifts of Christmas only last but a short time. But, the love and light of God is endless and everlasting, as reminded to us each and every Christmas."

—REV. JEFFREY R. TREXLER, Executive Director, Order of Malta, American Association

"Written with the imaginative wonder of childhood, seasoned by the weariness of adulthood, *A Child's Christmas in Williamsburg* is a Christmas story for our own age, an age troubled by disappointment and confusion, yet still hopeful for redemption."

—MICHAEL MARTIN, Director, The Center for Sophiological Studies

*A Child's Christmas
in Williamsburg*

A Child's Christmas
in Williamsburg

•

JOSEPH NICOLELLO

 Angelico Press

First published in the USA
by Angelico Press 2020
© Joseph Nicolello 2020

For information, address:
Angelico Press
169 Monitor St.
Brooklyn, NY 11222
www.angelicopress.com

ISBN 978 1 62138 655 1 pb
ISBN 978 1 62138 656 8 cloth
ISBN 978 1 62138 657 5 ebook

Cover design: Michael Schrauzer
Cover photo by Saunak Shah
(www.saunakspace.com)

All that is truely amiable is God, or as it were a divided piece of him, that retaines a reflex or shadow of himselfe. Nor is it strange that wee should place affection on that which is invisible, all that wee truely love is thus, what wee adore under affection of our senses, deserves not the honour of so pure a title. Thus wee adore vertue, though to the eyes of sense shee bee invisible.

Sir Thomas Browne, *Religio Medici* II: XIV

It was the resplendent eve of a prodigious day in little Sarah McGrady's life, Christmas Eve at seven years old in New York City, and her mother's glass lenses glowed somewhere near the still evening clouds, the still unseen tips of towers which scraped soundlessly the abstract sea-sky, reflecting the evening holiday display of FAO Schwartz beneath the cold colorless sky, alternating misty sequences of near-turquoise translucence in the early evening, where all of the people paraded about the disquieted one-way Avenues beneath a mirage of light, their faces aglow, or reflective, or breathtakingly sad and alone, walking the sidewalks desiccated with a lexicography of gum splotches and cigarette ends, Earth's capital from shop window to shop window, stop sign to stop light, and locked doors of libraries and the sweet scent of fried peanuts and steaming water breaking beside the subway entrances, all in one second, the next, where Sarah stood, window-shopping on this night arrived at last, her glowing eyes beneath the bath of multicolored Christmas lights, the old-fashioned round bulbs which did not blink but hover, her mother smiling suddenly and subtly, thinking private thoughts, memories of her mother who had died young from cancer, as she wept that morning, thinking, 'Because the spirit departed,' and a fragment of father practicing the religion of liquid oblivion, aspects of which had annihilated the soul of her own now-ex-husband, before surrogate mother Aunt May arrived so long ago, as she would tomorrow too, of this very street corner on this very day with this very beautiful young girl beside her, her first and last child, thinking she could tilt her head and hear the cathedral bells of 119th Street begin to resound, to clang and echo through melancholic time, to travel through the winding-down streets of palliated sleet, of icicle islands, passing through the vacant streets of Harlem with a pack of wild Rottweilers, men and women crying and laughing in the night, limousines which stretch and veer counter-clockwise, gleaming like sets of jet-black mirrors, those ashen storefronts caught within the soundtrack of sleigh bells, cathedral bells, the sun machine coming down on this year at last, let it end with peace, O Lord, or at least just let it end with Christmas, Christmas on Earth, the mother McGrady—proud beautiful young woman—squeezing gloved hands with her daughter, Sarah McGrady, Brooklyn girl, seven years young, smiling the tune of the towering piano keys, glass encasings of life-size electronic nutcrackers staring down through whiskers into the eyes of a dozen rosy-faced boys and girls, their parents beside them little more than rosy-faced boys and girls themselves, gusts of frozen foggy-breath against the dampened window-pane upon which to inscribe secretly with a twig or a gloved finger-tip one's initials, or Santa Claus, or a smiling face, glowing and dissolving amplification of light-blue streams of snowfall in the next window display, blanketed grounds of papier-mâché snowfall, surrounding towers of lamp-lit windows, families coming together again at last twenty-six stories in the New York dusk, the shadows which stretched out across fenced-in gardens of bare rose-buds, discarded wicker cabinets, toothless men from faraway lands who sat up all night upon stacks of freshly-printed newspapers drinking hot coffee and chocolate egg creams and eating crumbs of saltine crackers pinch by concentrated pinch, on the corner of a street whence singular tinsel bows were blowing down the yellow-checkered one-way street—but that, all of this, now, stepping from the toy Shoppe, but that was nothing, Caitlin McGrady sniffed, holding tight to her daughter's little hand—the beauty of Christmas Eve was not to her all that which happened each five seconds in the city, but the way those precious Christmas light displays within the shop windows nearly paralleled Sarah's sky-blue young girl eyes shining like diamonds, counterbalanced her dark brown hair held together by her favorite black velvet band, her miniature banana-yellow rain boots which went *clack-clack* against the dimmed street, Sarah then considered, something like the way reindeer tracks sound from a winter dream, one decades past, Caitlin considered, a dream decades past of a future something like this, the tonality of crisp cold air, winter dreams decades dissolved here now at last, lifting Sarah into her arms and walking down into the subway station through rising and falling and dissolving funnels of breath, and an old plump homeless man clanging bells together beside an old paint bucket filled with pennies, a frail dirty-blonde puppy tied to a post, the name Prancer inscribed on the mint-green collar upon its miniature shivering neck, his miniature nose the apparition of a wet, black bough, in the subway station on Christmas Eve.

Caitlin McGrady turned Sarah McGrady away from the man, his shivering puppy; for the girl, Sarah, had wanted nothing more than a puppy like that for years, and yet Caitlin could not afford one, nor could she hold out the suspense of tonight any longer. Her Williamsburg apartment disavowed pets of all sorts, anyway, she had told Sarah, at last.

"Mommy, look," peeped Sarah, blowing a stream of cold air at the convex mirror, "Don't it look like we all smoking?"

"Doesn't," Caitlin said, and with her free hand retrieved their Metrocard.

In a moment of silence Sarah caught wind of the man jingling the bells, the poor puppy beside him.

"Mommy! Look at the doggy! Wait!"

Caitlin sorrowfully swept through the crowd ascending the steps, ignoring her daughter just once, and Sarah held back tears of frustration and agony. She made a face and tried to get a glove off to throw into the crowd. But if she moved too much any which way one of the dozen brisk bodies before her was sure to knock her down. She held her mother tight, and tried to focus on all the window-shopping they had done that day, and when she could think of the puppy she could pout, drawing subtle attention to herself, eyes averting thereafter to the striking plain beauty of her mother, her delicate pale features never to be bothered by makeup.

"Why are you pouting, Sarah?"

She knew she could not mention the small puppy, for she would break into embarrassing hysterics, and so she thought awhile and changed the topic.

"I don't want to leave New York," she sniffed, wiping her face with gloved hands. "I don't want to go back to Brooklyn already. I hate it there."

"But we're only going downtown right now," Caitlin smiled, rocking her child in her arms. Sarah's sky-blue eyes lit up once more. "And we're going to see Daddy."

Then it was Caitlin's turn to cry, but she did not cry, and as Sarah spoke of the evening ahead she searched her mind for a better, less melancholic time: Christmas Day, and the party she was having in her miniature apartment on Grand Street. She rocked Sarah halfway to sleep and was glad to get a seat on the subway car with no trouble whatsoever.

With her thumb and index finger she straightened Sarah's hair with great, delicate concentration, pressing the dew-drops of dissolved snow out and trying to pay no mind to the eyes around her and Sarah sleeping, friendly as such attention may have been, it reminded Caitlin of obtrusive things, of the impossibilities of such transitions as explaining to your daughter once and then again how a Christmas without Daddy would be just as good as any other.

As the train slowed into the Spring Street stop Sarah's eyes opened wide at once, as if pulling herself from a dream. Her mother observed those delicate features as if looking through a scrapbook from her own childhood; the child went to explain the dream, her eye widening before rosy red wintertime cheeks, when the subway doors clicked open and the tambourines, harmonica, banjo and bass drum of a one-man band flooded in. They smiled at the man in his elf hat with his sped-up rendition of Rudolph the Red-Nosed Reindeer.

"Do you know where we are, sweetie?"

"Not in Brooklyn, I know, but I dunno this stop. What's Vandam Street?"

"Just wait," smiled Caitlin.

They walked out into the quiet evening upon 6th Avenue. Sarah eyed the nearby stands and towers with comprehensive determination, squinting and making the rounds.

"Well Mama, I can't tell, but it is New York!"

They walked down the quietest one-way street in all of SoHo, save perhaps Jersey Street—Vandam.

The hair school was closed down, the diner locking up, and all that stood alive between Caitlin, Sarah, and Varick Street was a dim bath of nostalgic light dancing from twig to turning twig, a nostalgia for the present, and marble walkway to a three-story brick-red apartment building.

"Close your eyes now," Caitlin said, and scooped Sarah up into her arms. She walked ahead half the block, recalling with a winter smile when as a child she had taken a holiday internship at the Playhouse, and of last weekend when she'd heard a limited run of a ballerina-skit would be playing through February. Aside from a puppy, there was nothing Sarah McGrady wanted more than ballet lessons, and more than once Caitlin had caught her daughter skimming again and again through old picture-books filled with her mother a mere ten years old, clad in various ribbons and bows commemorating her adolescent ballet achievements, and how a pretty of a girl she was.

She held her eyes closed, recalling that soon she would see her father for the first time in a long time. He was a rich man, Sarah knew, and he had a different pair of glasses each time they went out to lunch, and she disliked the way her mother acted around him. People change in front of other people, she had come to understand through school, but some people seemed to undergo metamorphoses—a strong, beautiful woman such as her mother seemed to go frail and nervous at each brief meeting between her and father. She thought, perhaps, that God had now reunited the two—Wait, didn't her father live somewhere around here, down one of these strange quiet streets of Manhattan?

"Now open them, Sarah!"

No, better than her father—her mother framed

and dressed in her ballerina outfit, on display in Manhattan! Coming soon!

"Mommy, that's you!"

"Well almost, Sarah, but how about we go see the show the day after Christmas? Just you and me, if I can get tickets?"

It was the sole thing aside from a set of ballerina shoes that could have rendered Sarah so overjoyed, so radiant, staring ahead to the poster on the quiet street.

She walked ahead to the glass encasing and put her small hand against the blinking light. No, that's not mommy after all, the little girl shrugged, sighed inwardly. Because mommy is prettier. But we'll go anyway! The day after tomorrow, the day after the family party!

"I don't want to see Daddy anymore," Sarah said, crossing a deserted 6th Avenue to Spring Street. "I want to go home and set everything up for the party."

"I thought you said you didn't want to go back to Brooklyn yet, little lady?"

The sounds from here to Houston Street, to Hoboken, settled down once and for all with the sun and for once and for all only, as real and recaptured as the air one breathes on Christmas morning when the city streets are fast asleep as a newborn child, still as primrose bouquets in Brownstone windows lit by candlelight, that surreal slumber of golden hours one inhales, exhales, yet can never photograph that feeling of a child's Christmas anywhere, particularly, here, now, on Broome Street, a place where to this day untold thousands of yearning aesthetes arrive only to emerge unknown, not unlike Heaven, where there must be every saint whom the church never had the chance to canonize, but who nonetheless subscribed to a Jerusalem of the soul, whereas in Williamsburg one is surrounded by anonymous bodies concerned less with the heavenly city than the prospect of heaven in a black leather jacket, rendering a sort of theological geography to the neighborhood's quest to move from a Mecca of the afflicted, to a pure and constant adjective.

"Don't you want a slice of pizza? You must be hungry at least!"

"I don't want stupid pizza," said Sarah, climbing across a mountain of snow blackened by exhaust and splashes of oil. At the top of the mountain she used her small hands as binoculars, searching out that stranger called her father.

The rare souls still outside stopped to marvel at the girl.

"God bless you," an elderly woman with pearls expressed shakily to Caitlin. "That girl's like a little angel—Merry Christmas to you, sweetheart—"

"I see him," Sarah stated to no one but the wind. "Come on, Mama, I see him."

James Toole, autodidact architect, stood tall and emaciated outside of the pizzeria in his best black blazer, a light beard, and freshly polished shoes.

The sight before him was the opposite of what it had been: The lady, the mother of his child, approached him with a casual smile, a forgiving smile, that seemed more fitting to belong to Sarah, where she, on the other hand, stepped toward him with

downturned miniature eyebrows, rain boots breaking across the ponds of slush. He knew both well
enough to know that this little scene was far more
spontaneous than planned, and contemplated the
effect of the two dirty martinis he'd had on
Broome Street—they had been strong, surely, but
not strong enough to exhibit such hurt in the eyes
of his child on Christmas Eve.

Regardless he dropped to his knee, smiling honestly to Caitlin—she was a beautiful young woman
and always would be, and something about her
poverty, to James, seemed to make her all the more
alive. It was not her fault he'd found someone else,
of course not, and yet he could not help but to per-
petually remind himself of everything that had
gone wrong when he saw the mother of his child
in person, more often appearing hurt than other-
wise, with bags beneath her blue eyes, and the ec-
stasies of that family he could never let dissolve
from his mind, each encounter amplifying the forever mixed feelings within his heart.

Sarah longed to say several things at once, and

right away, but found herself being hugged and kissed by her father, and all of the things she had wanted to say to him slipped away within his arms. She longed to cry, and felt her eyes burn, but convinced herself it was just because of how strong her father's cologne was, and not how honestly he loved her.

"Merry Christmas, Beauty Queen!" He picked Sarah up, and the girl watched over the passersby of Spring Street with a near-tear in her eye. She clamped her teeth down so hard her head began to shiver—but still, that was better than a thousand bitter tears.

James handed Caitlin a crisp, sealed envelope and rocked Sarah to and fro, inquiring as to what she'd asked Santa Claus for this Christmas.

They moved to the far end of the sidewalk, letting the people pass by in miniature parades, their hands holding tight to the wiry strings of multicolored tinsel shopping bags.

"Well, a puppy of course, and ballet shoes, and a couple of other things I probably won't get. And I asked for a couple of other things Mama said Santa couldn't bring because they weren't real."

They sat down to the warm pizzeria in a far corner, each with a slice of hot cheese pizza and a Coke. Caitlin listened to her daughter continue:

"Well, I mean I wanted one of those doll sets, you know, but with a different kind of doll house. Instead of a bunch of little things," she paused, watching in amazement the mass of steam rising from where she'd just plucked away a piece of cheese, "I wanted a big, big doll house the size of a mansion with all of the little bathrooms and twunny rooms and walked-in closets and a big old garage and cars for the dolls to go in, then a highway set kind of which went to the city, and a construction set of figures, see, because then for this year they could do construction and then by next Christmas Santa could bring a city for the dolls to play in when they got bored with the big old house and the town of big old boring houses like Uncle Jack's neighborhood and that was when Mama said that we could try, but Santa might not be able to make it. So I told her what everyone at school told me, that Santa Claus was fake."

Caitlin exhaled through her thin nose a sigh of rolled eyes, cueing James to take over.

"Don't listen to anyone that says that. Do you believe in God, Sarah?"

"Me and Mama prayed that God keep our hearts set aglow, that the Virgin Mary and her Mama, St. Anne, watch over us, and thanked the angels at our table for the chance to be alive."

"Indeed, not everyone has the chance to live. So you do believe in God?"

She looked up perplexedly at her Mama, then down nodding at her little shoes, recalling something her friend had said she had responded when a boy at school said 'Jesus was a man, and therefore couldn't perform miracles, and so what do you say to that?'

"That's a stupid question!"

"Then so is the Santa question!"

"Oh," Sarah shrugged, "Never thought of it that way."

"Would God not let Santa Claus exist?"

"No."

"Then there you go! Sarah, don't you know you're the prettiest and smartest girl in that whole school? Of course they're going to try to mess with you!"

Caitlin stood for the bathroom. Inside she opened the Christmas card, ran her eyes along the check for ten-thousand dollars. This would help them make it into the New Year.

Next, she texted her friend from the pet store on Berry Street and said she'd be dropping off the house keys in about an hour.

"Daddy," said Sarah, "I have to tell you something." For the first time that night she looked right into his eyes, then away.

"What is it, honey?"

"I'm not going to call you Daddy anymore. From now on I'm calling you Dad."

"Well alright, princess." He felt rotten about all of his life, all at once, his heartache italicized as he checked his phone for the time and knew he would have to return to Broome Street soon for his date. "I can't object to that, if it makes you happy." Sarah thought awhile:

"Well I dunno if it makes me happy, I guess, but it makes me feel more like a grown-up."

They embraced out on the street in the cold night, Caitlin thanking him once more for coming out, and making plans to get him and Sarah together after the holidays.

"All that bum lefted was card I can't even see now?"

"Sarah McGrady! Stop this right now! He said to open the card when you got home, and it's left— not *lefted*."

Ashamed at her grammatical blunder, Sarah walked silently again into the subway with her hands in her pockets, and she wanted to feel no way but frustrated, for she knew all that could help her now, on Christmas Eve, was to come up for air in Williamsburg—for that was always the grandest feeling of all, really, escaping that infernal city and back into the Brooklyn twilight.

Across the water Caitlin daydreamt of her past and of her future, of returning sometime soon to doctoral studies, to her days at Columbia, to the annual Christmas Day party tomorrow afternoon, of what James was to do tonight, of what her mother would be like tomorrow, and of how wonderful the food would be, and how happy Sarah would be to see her aunts and uncles once more, and this time all proud with a beagle puppy dog within her palms.

Sarah was thinking of their miniature Christmas tree, of attaining it out on 14th Street weeks prior with her mother, and of how foolish the children at school had been to not believe in Santa Claus. What was the point in that? she contemplated, as the emptied train slowed down, at last coming to a total stop.

Ladies and gentlemen we'll be moving again shortly just wanted to let ya'll know there's a train still in at next stop, Bedford Avenue, next stop, be moving shortly thank you.

"Mommy, is Aunt May coming tomorrow?"

"Yes."

"Yay!" peeped Sarah, cuddling again within her mother's arms. "Tell me that old story about Aunt May while we're waiting!"

"Oh, Sarah, I'm tired now—let it wait till later."

Poor girl, thought Caitlin, just waking up from a nap and I'm tired as a dog.

Sarah looked to her reflection in the subway window beneath a cavernous light. She clicked her yellow boots together and smiled, radiant until she noticed her mother deep in thought, focusing on some invisible object near the ground

When I was six, or seven, or four, or something surreal like that, there were the long weekends within which Aunt May used to come and pick me up from school, retie together my boot laces, and then we would walk through the autumn rain of Long Island as I spoke shyly of my day down to the most intricately unnecessary detail.

We would arrive at the old brick house, step silently up the staircase suffused with permanent traces of perfume and watch from a distance as my father and mother styled their hair and stamped out cigarettes. Till Aunt May touched my shoulder with her frail, spotted hand, I felt a

*stranger, or a ghost, and laughed gaily when at last my
mother turned to notice my presence, handmade binoculars
around my eyes, glancing about the kitchen from above
the old rickety barn door.*

"Do you mind if we walk a bit tonight? I've got
to see an old friend and wish her Merry Christmas
on Bedford Avenue," said Caitlin.

"I don't mind, Mommy," Sarah said, thinking of
holding her mother's hand, for her mother looked
so lost and sad and alone.

*Before my mother came to pick me up I would overlook
the jam-packed driveway of station wagons and dampened
leaves, of rainbow-streaked reflections tilting westward in
the October evening, that sunlit sky streaked with shades
of neon orange, electric pink.*

"*I don't want you to leave,*" *I cried, tossing my arms
around my mother's leg. "What if you never come back?*"

Sarah considered the people on the train could
have been staring at her mother but decided against
it. She didn't look all that sad, really, thought Sarah
McGrady, but I just sense it, I guess. I guess daugh-
ters can sense things in their mothers that no other

sort of combination of people can do. I guess Mama's thinking about something, and I don't know what to say.

We all laughed a bit, my father told me to shut up, and I pressed my nose against the light denim before I flung myself down the hallway and into the living room. The adults talked quietly for some time, and eventually Aunt May returned, taking off her long black coat and observing briefly an obscure photograph framed upon the pale-peach wall.

"Some day when you're older and in love, because you are dust, you'll understand, you'll go to the city for the weekend and have the time of your life but you don't want anyone else to come."

"Why not?"

Aunt May would turn her hazel eyes away from mine, disdainfully speaking something or another which upon memory seems to parallel the striking epilogue to a long-winded book of verse. Her voice seemed then as it seems now, a combination of glossy ancient wooden floorboards and paperbacks bound together by fresh coats of brush-on glue.

"Why don't we go to the pizzeria, then the bakery, then the video store? It's a beautiful night."

At least the train's moving now.

Aunt May and I seemed to have that sort of luck: It was always beautiful outside, and evening, when I saw her. It would have been mighty strange to see her in the daylight, the total daylight, wearing anything but her long black coat and always speaking, even of the present moment, in a middle-pitched past tense tone of voice, as though specific words and images were things she had forgotten at home upon the dining room table.

My parents came back in and spoke to both of us. I sat on Aunt May's lap and thought of her house in the countryside I had gone to once, with heads of hunted animals lining the walls. I was eating Butterfinger BBs and looking through the open automatic doorway into the porcelain bathroom, which contained a urinal taller than me. I had never seen one except at Yankee Stadium. I stepped away from the urinal and ate my chocolate and looked at all of the heads on the wall, the heads of bear and elk surrounding a jam-packed refrigerator. I began to cry.

"Mommy, are you OK?"

"Yes, I'm tired—please, let me be just for a minute—please, Sarah."

"What is it," said my mother. "What happened?" "I remembered all the animal heads," I wept, "and I don't want to."

After a while my parents took the train into Manhattan and Aunt May was in our bathroom putting on makeup. She didn't even need makeup, I always thought, but if you like to do something, you ought to do it.

I thought again of the animal heads, the trophies her husband had awarded himself. Luck—I had exhausted my tears, and luck, luck, luck, it was nighttime and a full moon. I stood by the window and watched the traffic and thought that every car has its own group of people in it and they're all living their own lives and that could be scary, but it could beautiful. I wanted it to be beautiful, I remember, because beauty takes time, and nothing worthwhile does not take time.

There was a banjo song on the radio and the neighbors were thrashing plates around. My stomach growled, in and out, like a rollercoaster, but I wasn't really that hungry. My stomach has exaggerated.

"*Ready?*" shouted Aunt May, twirling around with her rep lipstick and golden bracelet.

She helped me with my boots and my department store corduroy coat, and we walked down the narrow sidewalk of bare trees, their accompanying, towering shadows. I asked Aunt May how long it would take to walk to Manhattan.

"*Well we couldn't do that, but we could walk to Queens, I think, and take the subway from there. It would take a couple of hours, at least.*"

She spoke in an unguarded fashion which prompted me to believe I might have been onto something. I listened to our boot-heels click and clack. We walked by a big tree me and my dad once carved our initials into with an old pocketknife and I recognized the initials. They were getting old and sort of dissolving, but if you looked closely you could see them, like one of those Magic-Eye books.

It's not very often that people walk to Queens, of all places, in New York. Some of my family lived in Astoria and Woodside. I got to thinking we could visit them and spend the night and the next night and go to the big shop-

ping mall during the day to window-shop and laugh and eat the best food in great company and keep laughing.

I knew I was not like anyone else, even then, and felt bad sometimes when May got quiet at an intersection red light where no cars passed or paused. I never had a favorite color, or interests other than dinosaurs and locomotive trains, except baseball maybe, but Aunt May was so pretty she couldn't have watched baseball. I had about five thousand trading cards I could have told her about, but I didn't think it would matter all that much. I was thinking a lot, hypnotized by the perpetual monologue in my brain that seems to have been birthed by memory, when we rushed to the comic bookstore.

We held hands and walked past the tall marble Indian man smoking a pipe.

"Pow wow," I said.

"Pow wow," Aunt May smiled.

The store smelt of fresh ink, fresh tobacco, bubblegum-flavored chewing gum, and I used to like to borrow the shopkeep's butterfly-knife to cut the yellow cables off the unsold bundles of newspapers. I felt a sense of warmth within the presence of the magazine man, bearded and of-

ten disheveled, eating crumb cake and smoking cigarettes, listening to the greatest music of all on the portable radio— Indian music—and I always knew that when you listened to Indian music it was so good that you might never know the lyrics but just hear the chants and know that was life. The Indian food I'd had once or twice in Manhattan was excellent too, yet no one could pronounce the names properly in my family or make out the ingredients with confidence or build the courage as to inquire. But that was the charm of India, and I always wanted to go there one day, and perhaps live there, live a long time. But who cares about India when your daughter is undergoing her first fatherless holiday season. What did I do wrong?

"I wanted to walk, Mama," said Sarah. They ascended the stairs, through the turnstile, and out onto the becalmed street.

Caitlin took her daughter's hand and people-watched, walking against traffic down the Avenue. She wondered if she looked as young and beautiful as those young men and women walking by, and if so why had she been alone for so long now, sleeping alone, alone, for she knew it was right to feel beautiful but at times it all crashed down, and the soul was a mischievous, ugly thing, like hand-carved coffins, or unwatered flowers.

She broke cleanly from her daydreams as she walked right into a young man stepping down from the tavern doorway strewn with Christmas lights, and the young man's cigarette broke across the concrete, swept embers breaking in the cold wind to the other side of the street, trampled under black cab tire.

"Are you alright, ma'am?"

A young woman stepped out behind him, laughing, "William!"

Caitlin laughed, apologizing, and Sarah looked up at her mother, the young man and the young woman in awe. His mustache twirled neatly, nearly to the tip of his glass lenses, and when he caught the little girl staring at him he knelt down to her, placing his glasses upon his head whilst his friend, Sarah's mother, looked on warmly:

"Well you're just about the prettiest little girl I've ever seen," said William. "But always remember—what's her name? O, Sarah: honor thy mother and father. I wanted to take a moment from discussing how I intend to swallow the world whole through language and finish what Joyce started, but only for my relative, Shelley's friend, Dan Healy, and because I love life, and because the death of God is an interesting idea, but one that does not affect God, and because you—!—you are the prettiest girl I have ever seen!"

He looks so crazy he makes me smile, snorted little Sarah.

"What do you say," grinned Caitlin. All of life rushed with rose-red color back into her pale cheeks. Sarah looked at her, smiling also, because her mother no longer seemed apprehensive, and it felt like Christmas Eve all over again. Caitlin rejoiced and was glad that this man was with someone who must have been his girlfriend, or at least someone who from the shadows held his pale hand.

The Bard, the Sheik of Williamsburg, reached into his long black coat, removing a crisp dollar bill:

"Now beautiful Sarah, why don't you buy yourself a little treat tonight while you're out, before you go home to set out the cookies and milk for Santa?"

"And what do you say, Sarah?"

She reached out her small hand and accepted the bill:

"Thank you, mister."

William kissed her once upon the forehead, wished Caitlin his best holiday wishes, and turned back around in one motion and reentered the Greenpoint Tavern. For a moment a chorus of guitars and voice broke maddeningly onto the still wintry street.

"Well, wasn't that nice?"

"Yes, Mama."

A block from the pet shop Sarah stopped in her tracks, overlooking the last of a street vendor's display of old comic books and magazines. She decided to save her dollar.

"Mommy?"

"Yes?"

"Mommy, when I grow up I want to be as beautiful as you," Sarah said, in her small voice, which cracked slightly and beautifully then with spontaneous, honest love, "And even if Dad isn't around, we'll still have the best Christmas ever."

"You think so, my little lady?"

"Of course!"

Caitlin picked up Sarah and kissed her cold lips once, ran her nose over her daughter's rosy cheeks, and ordered two hot cocoas from the street vendor.

"Here honey—hold these, and it's very hot except the whipped cream, and just let me wish my friend Merry Christmas here next door."

Sarah watched her turn into the pet shop and felt sad but would not let it bring her down.

"Maybe next year," she thought aloud, "Maybe next-next-next years when we're not poor anymore, I'll have ballerina lessons and a puppy." She set her cups upon the cart's silver counter and took the crisp dollar bill from her pocket and smiled looking to the starless sky.

"All ready, Sarah?"

"And, and can we walk through McCarren's Park like the old days?"

Brett, Caitlin's friend from the pet shop, ascended the narrow, creaking stair-well to the third floor, turned the key, and set the miniature kennel beneath the Christmas tree. As directed, he took out a long slip of rose-red & mint-green wrapping paper, a silver bow, and sat down beside the tree with his phone out. He held the puppy, not much bigger than an infant's shoe, in his hands and smiled, signing the puppy Silver Bells, drinking merrily from his flask, and the puppy licked his cheek over and over with his miniature bubblegum-pink felt tongue.

"A little tongue like Milosz's early porch with battleships."

"What?! You live in another world!"

"Yes, indeed the poet does live in another world," said Brett. He waited around for Caitlin's text message, which signaled that she and Sarah would be arriving home in some ten minutes straight from the shops of Graham Avenue, and that all was running smoothly.

When he received the message, he tucked the puppy away, leaving holes for air, and listened to his tale wag with nervous slow-motion in the dark. He looked over the one-bedroom apartment and wondered aloud how any two people could live here, let alone throw holiday parties. He said a quick prayer for Caitlin, considered the fifty-dollar tip upon the chipped coffee table and left it behind, beside the couch, to acknowledge he'd seen the offering and had no use whatsoever for it.

When he set the keys beneath the floor-mat he marveled at the night sky, hailed a cab, and arrived in time to pull down the last aluminum shop barriers with his partner.

"All of that go well?"

"Her daughter will never forget this day, I think —it is the sort of day which makes hard times endurable, and the passage of time a beautiful thing, a natural thing—she says Sarah's wanted a puppy for three, four years! Imagine!"

The ring of keys was beneath the warped door-mat, as planned. Caitlin tossed the set up and down within her pale palm, recalling the paginations of Arthurian grails, spears of destiny; here was the last empirical anxiety vanquished on Christmas Eve, an attainment of the last key in the lock of Christmas, a light shining in the kingdom of shadows.

Sarah stood still beside the rusted gate of ancient bicycle locks and grills wrapped in torn tarps, looking ecclesiastically to the night sky, to the key turning in the lock. Through the slow reflection of the turning glass reflection of the door, she peered on tiptoe back to Grand Street, nearly vacant. Her two small grocery bags made rustling movements as she shivered, anticipating the heat of the hallway, her mother holding open the door and looking out upon the silent stoplight of the Grand and Graham intersection.

Mama and Dad were right, she thought, blowing out great gusts of foggy breath toward the radiant street-lamp. You should always believe in what you believe no matter if the entire world is against, because even if all of those billions of people I guess are against you, then, it actually wouldn't matter if you truly believed. Because there is a chance, I think, no matter how small, that everyone can always be wrong. How's anyone know anything about Santa Claus? I heard the sleighbells on the roof last year and all the other years—I always sleep with Mama on Christmas Eve, and wake up in the middle of the night a lot. She can't be getting up and making a big crinkling fuss of wrapped presents, eating cookies and drinking the milk in the nice glass we use—I know her handwriting anyways, and Santa Claus writes like a big, fat man, a great big fat jolly saint who never shaved. His cursive writing is fast I remember, but still very nice. When you read it you feel good—you know he came! I wonder how many pens Saint Nick goes through on an annual basis—well, Sarah, look at your grocery bags, look at the good pot-roast and potatoes and ginger-ale and egg nog and spices and everything you just bought on Metr'politan Avenues—how much food do they go through on a regular year? Or all of New York, or all of America, or all the world? See! Some things can't be proven because you either just know or you don't! Oh, and I can't wait to see Auntie May!

Caitlin watched the young girl, deep in thought, revisiting that crisp dollar bill the gentleman had given her. She thought of their long walk through McCarren Park, her dialogue on Santa Claus, and Sarah's ever-observant jubilation as the sea winds rushed through the park, sweeping over and through bare bushel swaying skeletons of trees, the holiday wind which chased them down Lorimer to Graham Avenue, and here they stood now, and what did the little girl know of what was in store for her! Be it the near future or the distant future: Time is Time, except on Christmas, when Time is so wonderful you could just cry cracking open your cobwebbed window just to taste the snowy air on Christmas!

"Come on, honey!"

Sarah spun right around as the young man had

done out on Bedford Avenue, and into the doorway.

"Mommy?"

"Yes?"

"Do I have to go to bed early tonight?"

"Well," taking the little girl's hand through tenement hallways of discarded picture frames and dropping tinsel and pine-needles of wreaths, "I thought that since it's just you and me we might stay up late and wait for Santy Claus and drink hot cocoa and watch the TV specials—what do you say?"

Sarah's face glowed with sudden bliss counteracting with the long day of walking and talking and going everywhere at once and walked beside her mother speechless.

They stood outside of the door, listening to a faint swishing sort of sound.

"Put your ear to the door, Sarah—Do you hear that?"

Sarah thought all at once that it sounded like the excited tail of a puppy dog. She thought of Sherlock Holmes, the picture book they'd read in school; she was Mrs. Sherlock Holmes, and onto something.

Yet she knew to not kid herself and instead studied the framed weeping willow trees upon the wall next to the dusty, unused coat rack and told her Mama she was crazy.

"I'm cold! I don't hear anything!"

Caitlin took her by the hand and into the bare apartment. She noticed at once the money moved yet remaining. Her heart glowed with the prospect of Brett's charity, and for her Christmas was complete—its soundtrack being the sudden infantile cry coming from the glittering, miniature wrapped box, or kennel.

"Mommy…" said Sarah.

She let go of her mother's hand and tip-toed, as if sleepwalking, to the wrapped box. Caitlin absent-mindedly walked to the bedroom, removed her coat, smiling inside, and walked back outside, casually aloof.

"Mommy, what is that?"

"Go ahead and open it, dear—did—oh, now I

see—you know sometimes Santa does come early when he's got a lot to drop off!"

She was right, Sarah shouted inside her imagination, this wasn't here before! I admit—sorry, God—that I snooped around in the closets! I never saw—

Sarah knelt beside the wrapped rectangle as the swishing sound increased. Her heart leapt out of her chest, and without permission she tore the wrapping paper to shreds, never bothering to unbutton her coat, or remove her rubber boots, whilst Caitlin turned up the heat two notches with a tear of joy in her eye.

"A puppy!" screeched Sarah, "A little Beego puppy!"

Dear Sarah Mirielle McGrady, read the note: *May you have a Merry Christmas and a Happy New Year, little chord of light; honor your mother, and love God forever and I shall take care of thee for infinite Christmases, Christmas on Earth*—Signed, Saint Nick.

O Brett, laughed Caitlin—only a part-time bookseller would—

"Help, mommy! Get the gate!"

Caitlin rushed to the kennel. Any sense of premeditation left her when she saw the small brown-patched white puppy dog, its microscopic whiskers, its coal-black, watery nose the size of a marble. Sarah's small hands shook with happiness.

Caitlin stepped to the kitchen and poured a glass of chilled Charles Shaw Chardonnay.

Mommy's having a glass of wine, Sarah sang in whispers to the puppy at last within her hands, laughing hysterically as—He? She? O, He—licked at her face, his little tail wagging maddeningly back and forth across her knee-high rubber rain boots.

What is a miracle if it happens every day, Caitlin considered:

Nothing!

A season in Hell has ended, at last, and this wine tastes better than the $1,300 champagne poured out at our wedding!

A sorrowful siren echoed vacantly across Bushwick Avenue as Sarah ran full speed to her mother and threw her arms around her. The puppy followed behind, observing everything at once, as Caitlin watched the old and young men alike smoking outside of the single bodega still open, the newspaper man arriving with the new edition, and snipping the yellow cables with a glistening pocket-knife.

"Mommy, mommy, what will we name him!"

"Whatever you like," Caitlin smiled, kneeling down to embrace her daughter once more. She kissed her strongly upon the lips. "Whatever you like, Sarah McGrady, whatever you like at all!"

She sent Brett a message of thanks and turned her phone off for the night. That year had been a long century.

The puppy dug at the tile floor in the kitchen with increasing passion. Caitlin and Sarah watched the shadows of his miniature paws flay across the dimly-lit kitchen walls.

"We'll name him Crouton! Crouton! And Mama, can he sleep with us tonight!"

"Of course!"

Ten minutes later Sarah was fast asleep in her holiday jammies with Crouton sound-asleep at her side. Caitlin watched them a moment, set out the milk and cookies, and the presents for Sarah, Aunt May, and the rest. She had an extra glass of wine alone beside the window, and at midnight it was Christmas Day. She exhaled tearfully, sniffled, and clenched her teeth to stop, as she wanted to wake neither Sarah nor Crouton.

"How long I've waited for sanctuary," she cried, and before long she was fast asleep, too, somewhere between Sarah and the newborn puppy, somewhere beneath the dreaming moon.

Sarah awoke at the crack of dawn, tip-toed out of bed and peeked through the dusty blinds: neon orange streaks breaking across the light-gray frozen sky, the still streets of Christmas Day. She shivered out of thermostat and anticipation. She looked upon the locked store fronts of Grand Street, the canonical array of illegible graffiti, the barren corner where just tomorrow the empanada man would rise again, and just after today it would be a whole 'nother year till Christmas.

Aunt May, Uncle Watt, Scottie, Aunt Ali! I haven't seen them since Easter Sunday!

She tip-toed once, twice, and still her mother lay sprawled, fast asleep angelic. Crouton weaved through the puzzle of blankets, brushing his small body off at the edge of the bed. Sarah took him in her hands and kissed his nose once and again.

Then the puppy sneezed. "Shh, Crouton, you'll wake Mama!"

But then Mama was up, if only for a moment, and while she said nothing Sarah knew better than to leave the room. She took Crouton back beneath the covers and petted him for an hour. She wondered when Mama would want to take him on his first walk, what streets they'd walk down, and what else Santa brought her.

The doorbell rang once, twice, and again—there was the fresh smell of a dozen spices and scents in the air, the smell of a holiday feast. Sarah sat straight up in bed, alone, and instinctively looked through the old blinds. Judging by the slanted, nearly invisible sun, it was somewhere around noon, and she changed at once into her black dress with white bows and bolted straight through the bedroom and into the kitchen.

Aunt May took Sarah into her arms at once whilst Uncle Watt hollered and shouted about nothing anybody recognized, up the uncarpeted flights of stairs. He wore his beige size-42 corduroy suit, and a golfer's cap, whilst Cousin Scott—Watt's son and two months older than Caitlin—walked through the doorway looking his usual ashamed, sleepless way, in a navy-blue sports jacket, jeans, and a pair of black leather penny loafers with white socks. Aunt Ali, all six feet of her, walked in without cap, her dyed chemicalized crown, extravagantly-curled golden-blonde hair going this way and that, yet frozen, like Medusa's mugshot, and she shouted to the tune of the half-dozen other great heartfelt greetings, and all the while Aunt May—in her signature old lady's perfume, somewhere between an old person's house and a hazy packet of pumpernickel bread, swayed to and fro with Sarah held tightly, kissing her repeatedly on the forehead and singing:

I met a man who lives in Tennessee
And he was headin' for Pennsylvania
And some homemade pumpkin pie
From Pennsylvania folks are travelin' down

Meanwhile, Crouton traced circles around everyone and eventually Sarah noticed all of the presents under the tree. There was a whole bunch of them, but most of them were brought by the party-members, and while Sarah McGrady loved old May, Watt, Scottie, and Ali, they didn't usually come up with the best presents.

"That's alright," she said to Crouton, holding him up to the uncovered lightbulb beside the fireplace, "Because I got you, now, finally!"

The egg nog went around as the afternoon burned down, and poor Scottie carried on with his traditional vitriolic opinions on modern politics. His wiry face grew red at once, and only Uncle Watt could talk him out of it.

"How come Scottie gets so mad whenever I see him?"

"You'll understand someday," Aunt May

smiled, running her liver-spotted hand through the child hair. Ali and Caitlin, in another far corner, raved together of the restaurant in Hoboken everyone had attended for Easter Sunday dinner.

"Ali's funny," Sarah whispered, "She looks like one of those ladies that you see in the movies from Hollywood. She has the big gold earrings, the stockings, the fancy coats she wearses," pausing, then realizing that her grammar had been incorrect and that she ought to be corrected.

"She's always wearing them things," Aunt May whispered. "Maybe one of these days she'll find a husband."

Sarah stared at Ali's hair, listened to Uncle Watt speak at length with Scott, and thought there was something about her hair that would never allow her to get married. She looked at her mother beside Ali and felt proud.

"Did you get to see Daddy for Christmas?"

"Oh I saw Dad for a little while yesterday, he said Hullo in Manhattan. I had more fun with Mama. We went to Fayo Shorts and looked at the

47

lights, and window shopped, and took the train, and it was good and then we got home, home see, and Santa left Crouton while we were out!" She turned her ecstatic watery eyes to Aunt May, leaping from her lap, and taking the floor. "All the kids in school said no Santa existed but I knew they were wrong!"

After Aunt May told her the tale of The Little Drummer Boy beside the Christmas tree, Sarah got to talk to Uncle Watt and Scottie, then Ali, and after a while the feast of smoked duck, mashed potatoes, sweet potatoes, cabbage, and side-dishes of Uncle Watt's traditional glazed-ham was ready to eat. Everyone held hands and prayed to the Lord, Caitlin offering a song she had heard back in university on an Easter retreat to the Abbey of Gethsemane, a refrain that had never quite left her, and a prayer she could sing around neither husband nor friends, but family alone:

… The God who was and is to come—at the end, of the ages…

As they made the rounds Caitlin observed Watt and noticed how much he looked like John Candy. She had been wondering whom Uncle Watt had looked like forever. Now she knew, sneaking Crouton a small piece of ham, which he took and trotted away to the Christmas tree with. Sarah watched him, enraptured, and ate her dinner so fast as to begin opening presents before it was dark again.

Last Christmas, Sarah recalled, she had begun to notice a sort of special treatment of Scott McGrady. His extra-thick glass lenses had always sort of accompanied his towering emaciated figure in an intimidating, albeit unspeakable, sorrowful state. She always felt sorry for Scottie, maybe because he had always lived at home, or that he never left the house without Uncle Watt, enhanced by the sort of unspoken element accompanying his peculiar presence.

As the peach cobbler was being placed in generous slices where dinner plates had just been, Sarah felt Crouton at her feet, and went to retrieve him, to set him upon her lap, when Scottie reached for the wine bottle, slurring a characteristic abstract sentiment, presumably, to himself. She watched his suit jacket—which he never removed—ride up his long, stretched arm, revealing an array of pinkish scars across his right wrist.

"Scottie," said Sarah tenderly, looking for this first time that evening into his eyes, or toward the thick lenses separating their eyes, all the while acknowledging she had never given Uncle Watt's son a kiss Hello before.

"Yes," he slurred, "Pretty girl?"

He took a long pull from the bottle of wine before even pouring a glass—he took up the glass in his pale, shaking hands, and repeated his words in a trembling tone.

"What's that lines all on your arm there from? Did somebody scratch you?"

The forming conversations came to a halt. Scottie swallowed gravely, and as he tilted the bottle to his wine glass, dropped the glass, which shattered along the floor. He held his chin within his hand

and began to rock to and fro. Crouton stopped wagging his tail as the formulating conversations dissolved about the dinner table.

He swept up the bottle of wine, almost purposely revealing his scars this time, before Uncle Watt took his son's hand away. He let his dessert sit whilst Aunt May patted Sarah's knee beneath the tablecloth, and for some unknown reason Sarah felt too ashamed to look at Aunt May, or Ali, or even her mother. The sudden silence about the room felt suffocating, ominous even, and Sarah crossed her fingers that it would soon end. Uncle Watt walked Scottie to the fireplace.

"We'll load up the firewood now, Scott, and let the ladies enjoy their dessert!"

The way Scott hobbled out of the room seemed to fix itself then and there into Sarah's forming mind, and it seemed the precise static moment within which one has witnessed an unexplainable suffering forever, at which point those in the know can at last begin to wonder why something hadn't been done sooner by means of instruction.

Joseph Nicolello

"She's just a girl," smiled Ali, patting Caitlin on the arm, Caitlin whose face then seemed as if made of stone, sorrowful stone, within such a mind which then contemplated its grasp on reality, and childhood, and holidays, and poverty, and the cuts on her delicate hands grown coarse from over-working, that obscure flurry of suddenly definite despair which may strike any thinking person at random, oft with temporary or long-term paralytic effect, that face which then, eventually, through seconds of silence which sifted like quicksand in the colors of the mind, Aunt May spoke:

"She's not just a girl," Aunt May boasted, "But Sarah McGrady's the most beautiful girl I've ever seen in my life—and that, of course, she gets from her dear mother, my daughter."

At sundown Caitlin lit a stick of cinnamon-dipped incense and let it burn beside the Christmas tree. The coal in the fireplace had burnt out and Sarah had taken to playing a fortress-sort of game with Crouton, interweaving throughout her restructured maze of small and large wrapped boxes, sharing with the puppy some crumb of peach-cobbler each time he made his way out without whining.

"I wonder," thought Sarah, "Since the puppy knows, or I think he knows, that I am his Mama, or his Master, now, but he doesn't have a language or anything, I guess, he just sort of, all dogs just sort of live forever, so do humans too? Is there some power above us we know of, but cannot share the language with? Maybe God, I guess, but what about Mother Nature, or the sun? That old Ms. Ghiberti in science glass says we only uses 10 percent of our brains—is there something above us that useses all of it? I wish I was a puppy running around a maze, but then again, I guess I am. At least it's Christmas!"

"Shall we have Ms. Sarah McGrady handle the ceremonies," sang Caitlin, as she and Ali waltzed into the room. Aunt May followed, talking and smiling with Scottie, whilst Uncle Watt unbuttoned his enormous flannel shirt, swept crumbs from his neat-trimmed beard in the adjacent handheld mirror, and went on to devour the rest of the cookies and ice cream.

"Come on, Uncle Watt!" cried Sarah, the puppy at her foot wagging his miniature tail like a whip against discarded wrapping paper.

"Oh I'm-a comin' a comin' just now, sweet-heart!"

Watt yawned beside the window, overlooking the vacant streets, and smiling he turned to take his place within the small living room.

When it came time to divide the presents up, the once-mountainous array of boxes seemed to have shrunk dramatically in size.

"What's twelve, no, fifteen, sixteen divided by six? Gee!"

It reminded her that her family was poor, that Mama might never go back to school and might work instead, that Aunt May and Ali and Watt and Scottie all shared the same quaint, broken-down two-story home in New Jersey, and that none of the boxes that earlier could have been her grandly-designed doll-house seemed to match up. Sarah felt like her mother all of a sudden, trailing off into deeper thoughts than she ought to have on Christmas Day—that she ought to save such trivial little thoughts for the Sandman, for bed before school in the morning.

"Here, Scottie." Little Sarah handed him his three packets, and avoiding his eyes, his arms which concealed some scarred story she may never know, nor care to know. She observed his old-man shoes, unpolished, upon the wooden floor. She glanced at each hole in the sole of his decrepit shoes as he tapped his foot up and down, the way old-fashioned ladies do at big concerts in the black and white movies at the organs and the pianos in the boring movies Mama used to watch sometimes.

The first gift, from Caitlin, was a boxed set of books Sarah could not make out. She thought she heard somebody say Willum Shake Ear, but she focused more on Scottie's smile—one of the two or three times she'd ever seen him smile. He coughed a broken cough and handed the collection of books to Uncle Watt.

Scottie's next present was a box of cigars, the

prospect of which seemed to please him well enough.

The final package contained a shoebox, within which sat a sparklingly-polished pair of jet-black wingtip shoes.

"Like Daddy!" thought Sarah; and poof: Scottie was a new man. He stood, threw his old shoes in the garbage to a boisterous round of applause, and returning in his fresh shoes, knelt to kiss Sarah on the forehead.

The stubble scraped her, but she didn't mind—there was a moment wherein she thought to tell poor Scottie she loved him, but could save that for Easter Sunday—instead, she piped, "Merry Christmas to you, Scottie!"

Moving counter-clockwise, Caitlin came next. She received a beautiful sky-blue dress hand-quilted by Aunt May, a set of pots and pans—desperately needed—and a collection of the old movies she loved.

"Mommy, who is Josef von Sternberg?"

Caitlin grinned clutching onto her daughter's

small hand and taking a sip of hot cocoa. Sarah could tell by her face that Mama was happy, very happy, and went over the fabric, over the dress again and again with Aunt Ali, who received a fine collection of gifts whilst Uncle Watt sang in his trademark, thunderous, albeit melodious, baritone:

> *You'll hear Silver bells, silver bells*
> *It's Christmas time in the city*
> *Ring-a-ling, hear them ring*

Aunt Ali tore apart her wrapping paper with the zest of a fanatical child. Crouton ran through the debris, helping tear it apart further to an approving chorus of laughter, as a cheerful Ali unveiled an extensive makeup kit, a box of chocolate shaped like a heart, an avocado-green handmade dress identical to Caitlin's, and a charcoal portrait drawn by Scottie.

Uncle Watt stood as Sarah rushed over his presents and insisted along with the adults that the aging man sit down. He received with enormous pride that enormous flannel coat, a pair of spiraling golden-black hunting boots, and a collection of old-fashioned records, perhaps ten, Sarah thought, in all.

"But I threw out my record player long ago! Ah, perhaps hang them up in frames upon the wall— Oh, John Denver!"

Caitlin stood to help Sarah lift one of the last and heaviest boxes.

"Help Uncle Watt unwrap that box, sweetheart," said Aunt May.

Sarah didn't understand why anyone would want a brand-new record player, or who made them, or anything like that, but the look in Uncle Watt's eyes said enough. He stood, extending bear hugs with such gargantuan rapidity that the puppy began to run in great circles, wheezing and sneezing, batting its dampened, glistening coal-black nose.

"Well it's alright, Mama," thought Sarah, "Because Crouton is, really, enough, I know. When the kids bring everything to school, I'll make something up, or bring in a picture of Crouton! I know a puppy's expensive and Santa's in a hurry! I walked by the pet shop once—puppy costed four thousand dollars!"

Aunt May took with delicate care the wrapping paper from her presents, lips pursed, and Sarah looked at the old lady with marvelous pride. She looked ahead to Easter Sunday once more, to take the train across the train out to hum-drum New Jersey, to sit in the old wicker chair in the old house that forever smelt something like a café in the wee morning hours, Aunt May with her fresh cinnamon buns, hot chai in those hand-carved porcelain cups Uncle Watt had made in high school, the scones topped with melted vanilla cream, the octagonal leaf-green dish centerpiece upon the long kitchen table, always filled to the brim with hard candies from Holland, which melted in one's mouth with the dissolving taste of toffee.

Aunt May's false teeth shone like little electronic candles, unraveling the brand-new, voluminous cook book, the set of Indian teas bought in Union Square, the hand-stitched box of imported, encapsulated spices bought from an eyeless street vendor in Red Hook, and lastly, the photographic collage book Caitlin and Sarah had assembled together containing a chronology of the McGrady family, from the late 19th century straight through to Sarah's first taking of the Holy Communion. There was stillness about the room, like a misplaced man upon stilts, then, as Aunt May began again to speak, speaking in her brass-bright baritone, of the way candy tasted down Christmas Morning some decades past upon Houston Street.

An extension of my feelings, I continue to reconsider, that there is nothing more natural than imagining yourself another, when the snow falls slowly through just past one's glass back sliding door, and one recalls driving down the highway much younger with many friends as the sunlight came across one's eyes beneath the surrounding forestry of southern California, or Vermont, or Clinton, New Jersey, and if one had the energy, or the discipline, to peel his eyes open, one would see what serenity such light snowfall is, light falling down in slow-motion, now, where Uncle Watt is singing with his cigar beside lamplight, 'My central nervous system's been blown to smithereens!'

Dear old fat man, with the fingers of a plump pianist, and Scottie, God help Scottie, his soul set to infernal theocratic punctuation, life dissolving in the nonexistent air like ash, like ash, I say, over and over again, like ash we sift through this alphabetical delirium, redeemed by little more than the shadow of a puppy-dog's small feet trotting ferociously across uncarpeted floors, yes, then, for this, as Aunt May subsides, let my future be one of triumph, and if not my own, dear Lord, then let my Sarah triumph in this world—let her come into womanhood with a smile on her face, let her prosper with shimmering beauty, and let us all, here and now in this room, die with smiles on our faces after all, to the skull-crest canyon sea where I prayed for my mother, on Christmas Day in the morning—

After something of an eternity which spanned five or six seconds, or, say, six or seven lifetimes, it was Sarah's turn to open her presents—alas, just one box remained. Scottie tilted his arm across the carpet to retrieve and hand the tight-wrapped box of golden bows and maroon-blue lines to Sarah.

She tore at the box whilst Crouton's tail smacked at the ancient black rocking chair leg like the wicked witch from woe-begotten films smacking out the dust from her broomstick, green-faced and all, yet gone, evaporated.

"Gosh," Sarah thought, tearing through the multilayered ambiguities, "I've seen these in the corner store before. It's a box in a box in a box. It's stupid as a Chinese finger-trap. But I still got my puppy. Crouton, come here, I love you funny little boy!"

Through three layers of torn green velvet wrapping-paper Sarah came to the shoebox. Within the shoebox she came to a polished pair of ballerina shoes. She felt the smiles around her shine down on her soul like honey. She slipped into the shoes—felt some sort of misplaced paper.

"Mama!" she cried, leaping into Caitlin's lap, "Tickets! Four tickets! To the *Met*! To the *Playhouse*!"

I remember when I was young, young as her, she, Sarah, I, Caitlin, once the family was something we could believe in amidst the midnight of the soul, O return to the roots, the McGradys.

Sarah stepped ahead through the hallway for her

dash of egg nog, her ballerina slips clicking quickly by tiptoe to the light of torn candle-lit curtains.

And I remember when Scottie could see, when he was not legally blind, when he was a handsome young man not yet destroyed by society.

Where the mahogany sound echoing at once through the still kitchenette once cloudy with twirling smoke of cataloged conversations.

And I remember Uncle Watt when he was thin, and I remember spending Christmas Eve with him in Harlem, and I remember Ali before she became a spinster, poor girl, she's never even realized what it's come down to, like snowflakes falling through the universe unto Earth, each layer of makeup another dreamt-home heartache, swallowing sad in the phantom of another year.

For all froze at once like icicles, the adult minds in silence before turning to go, Sarah McGrady skipping down the barren bare hallway, the miniature ballet tiptoes to go on forever unspoken save the next millennia, there where the future's imminent, reflective holiday solicitudes could prompt one at random to remember, to remember the sweet sadness, poverty upon Christmas Day in the evening.

She leaps into my arms the way I once leapt into Aunt May's; I hold onto her tightly; she is my only child, my daughter, my self.

After the party Caitlin took to sweeping up the house where Aunt May had missed, sending text-messages every which way concerning plans for the New Year and beyond, whilst Sarah slept sound-asleep in her holiday dress and ballerina shoes upon the old couch, Crouton nestled within her peaceful motionless arms, Caitlin all the while exhausted. She turned the volume down on the television set, turning straight to her collection of old black and white films. She removed the plastic-wrapping bit by bit, subduing her impulse to tear, and watched over Sarah out of the corner of her eye.

Halfway through the film, *The Docks of New York*, Sarah turned slowly, saying:

"Mama, I saw a woman outside of the window. But I dunno if it was a dream, but I never saw a woman all alone as that, and then she started running and running through the snow all by herself and then I woke up."

"Go back to bed, sweetie; we've got a big day tomorrow—remember, the show!"

Sarah closed her eyes and began to breathe deep breaths, as if at once falling right back asleep, yet all the while she had been awake and would remain awake all night, dreaming, simply dreaming, of what old people were like when they were young, of where all the taxi-cabs driving down Grand Street were heading, of how Santa Claus knew she wanted those ballerina shoes so bad she'd sleep with them on forever, and if dogs went to Heaven, and if after Mama fell asleep she could sneak a bowl of ice-cream with rainbow sprinkles and in the meanwhile listen to the classical symphonic soundtrack to Mama's movies, whilst the black and white shadowy light projected across her conquered eyes, like the snow rushing down in the vacant street, and before long she would be asleep and dreaming, as if she weren't already, Sarah smiled, and when Caitlin came to retrieve her, to change her into

comfortable clothing, Sarah still fought uncon-
sciousness, the inevitable, but then it came, tranquil
and natural like a summer afternoon, and the last
thing she remembered was the black and white
light coming across the Christmas tree like head-
lights from the streets below, and Crouton nestling
right beside her, and Mama kissing her once good-
night on the forehead, whispering her brisk prayers,
and tomorrow would be the day after Christmas in
Williamsburg, and it would be time, sweet time
once more, to begin counting down the days, the
hours, the months, the seconds, until Christmas
Eve came back again and all was well, thought Sarah McGrady, when all was ethereal, with the cine-
matic light like a harmonious flurry of snow, where
all was well, as beggar-children cried out in the
echoing nocturnal street of sleet-swept bliss, like a
song without words, little Sarah McGrady smiled,
on Earth as it is in Heaven, on Christmas Day as it
is in Williamsburg, Brooklyn, the life, the love, the
lost, alas, alack, alight, along, yonder is as yonder
'twas. All that shall be ends up as what was, as the

last window seals closed above a beggar who, having staggered in across the bridge from the Bowery, the last of his friends to die, singing, "Hark thy herald! Tis I, Father Moritz! I am Don Quixote! After you, after me, after virtue!" Caitlin stood at the window smiling, sipping a glass of wine; she recognized this disheveled man, who claimed he was a defrocked priest, condemned for his fidelity to the gospel, while others maintained his name was simply Frederick, and thus the Fr., or 'Father', was in fact the ravings of a madman. But was not the bible itself, she thought, a book all about madmen? And as she turned counterclockwise, contemplating revisiting Joseph Frank's magisterial five-volume biography of Dostoyevsky, to find that passage once again about what the author had said regarding what persons would do today should the Lord indeed return—

But then she was all at once falling asleep, as that strange voice below carried up through the echo of disintegrating arctic fog and rattling, rust-lined pipes, a nocturnal voice at once ascending and submerged within the streetlight vapor, strange liturgical chants oscillating up toward contained rooftop laughter and its cranial recollections atop the Williamsburg building, the night voices colliding into one distended representation, out racing into last clouds cast in the dream of a shadow of pipe smoke, into the dialogical sky of Christmas night, then way out, beyond the cosmos, at the threshold of perception, a choric genesis and structure.

Grand Army Plaza Library, Brooklyn
December 21–23, 2015

About the Author

JOSEPH NICOLELLO is the author of several forth-coming books written in his early and mid-twenties before turning his aesthetic interests into a life of scholarship, research, and professing. He is the author of a three-volume *Künstlerroman* forthcoming late 2020/ early 2021 (*Until the Sun Breaks Down*, 1,450 pages, Wipf and Stock Publishers), as well as a non-fiction text on Flannery O'Connor's literary theory, Jacques Maritain, and medieval philosophy, forthcoming from Angelico in 2021. *A Child's Christmas in Williamsburg* is the first installment of the *New York City Novella Tetralogy*: Brooklyn/Winter, Queens/Spring, Bronx/Summer, Manhattan/Autumn.